Mrs. Fitz's Flamingos

For Betty and Jimmy McCloskey:
my mother, who is like Mrs. Fitz,
and my father, who tells a good story

First Edition 1 2 3 4 5 6 7 8 9 10

Library of Congress Cataloging in Publication Data

McCloskey, Kevin, Mrs. Fitz's flamingos / by Kevin McCloskey.
p.   cm. Summary: To improve her view, a Brooklyn apartment dweller buys flamingos at the
five and ten cent store and displays them outside her window.   ISBN 0-688-10474-6.
ISBN 0-688-10475-4 (lib. bdg.) [1. Flamingos—Fiction. 2. Brooklyn (New York, N.Y.)—Fiction.]
I. Title. PZ7.M47841419Mr 1992 [E]—dc20 90-22788 CIP AC

Mrs. Fitz's Flamingos

By Kevin McCloskey

Lothrop, Lee & Shepard Books   New York

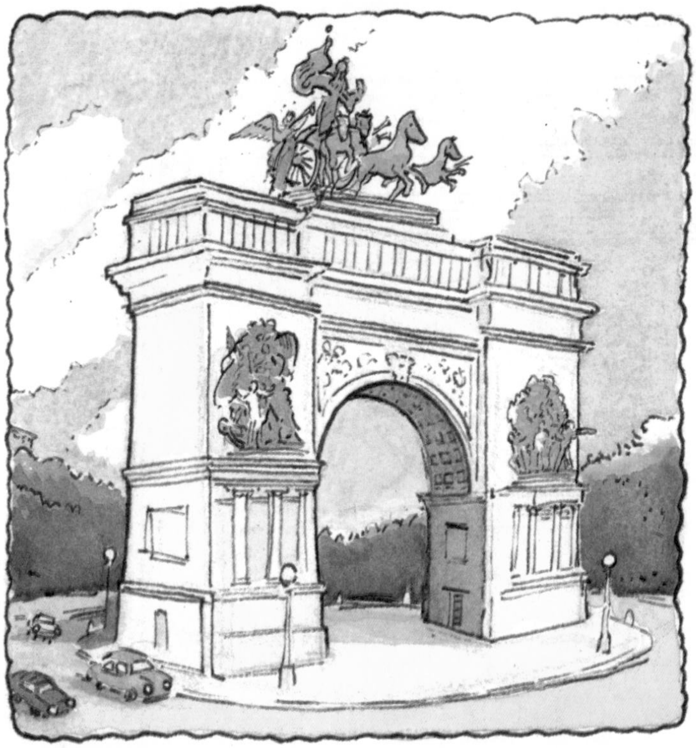
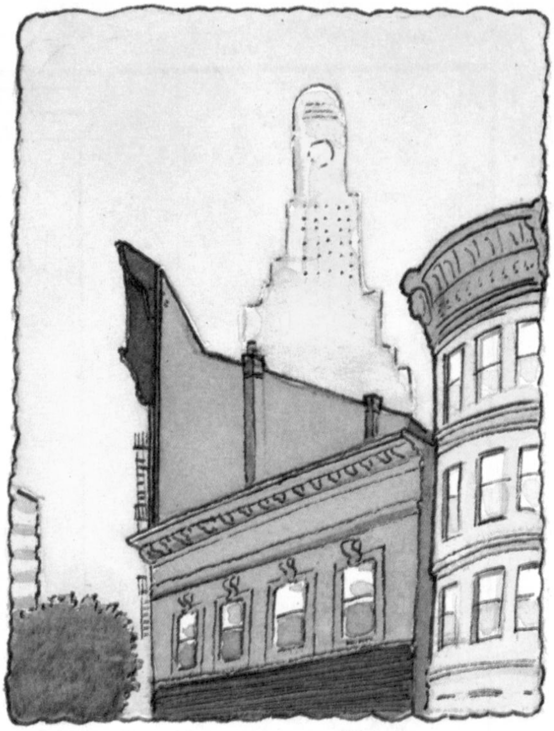
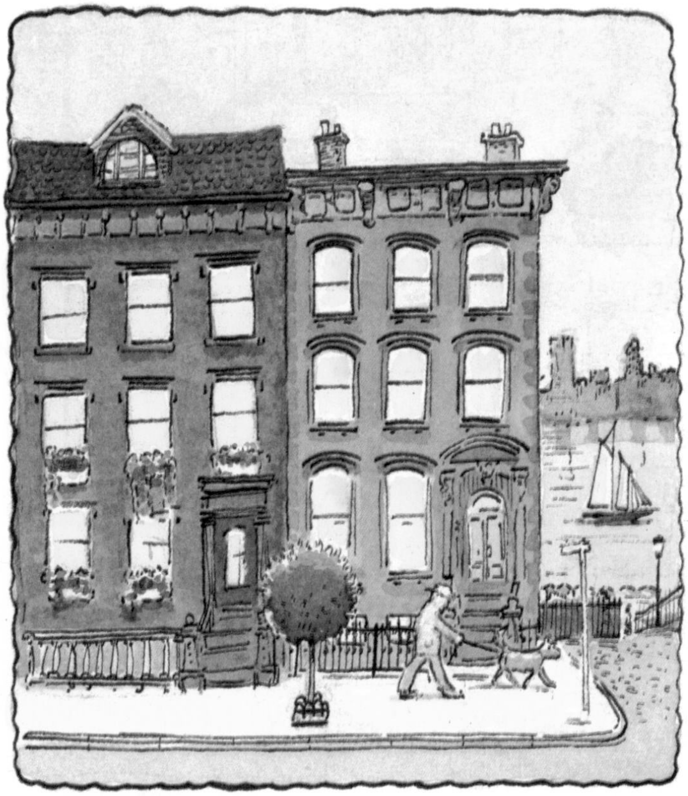
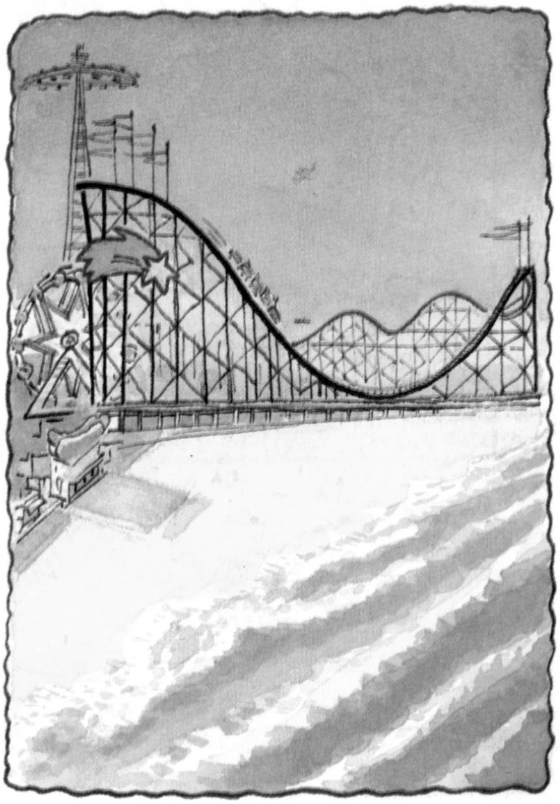

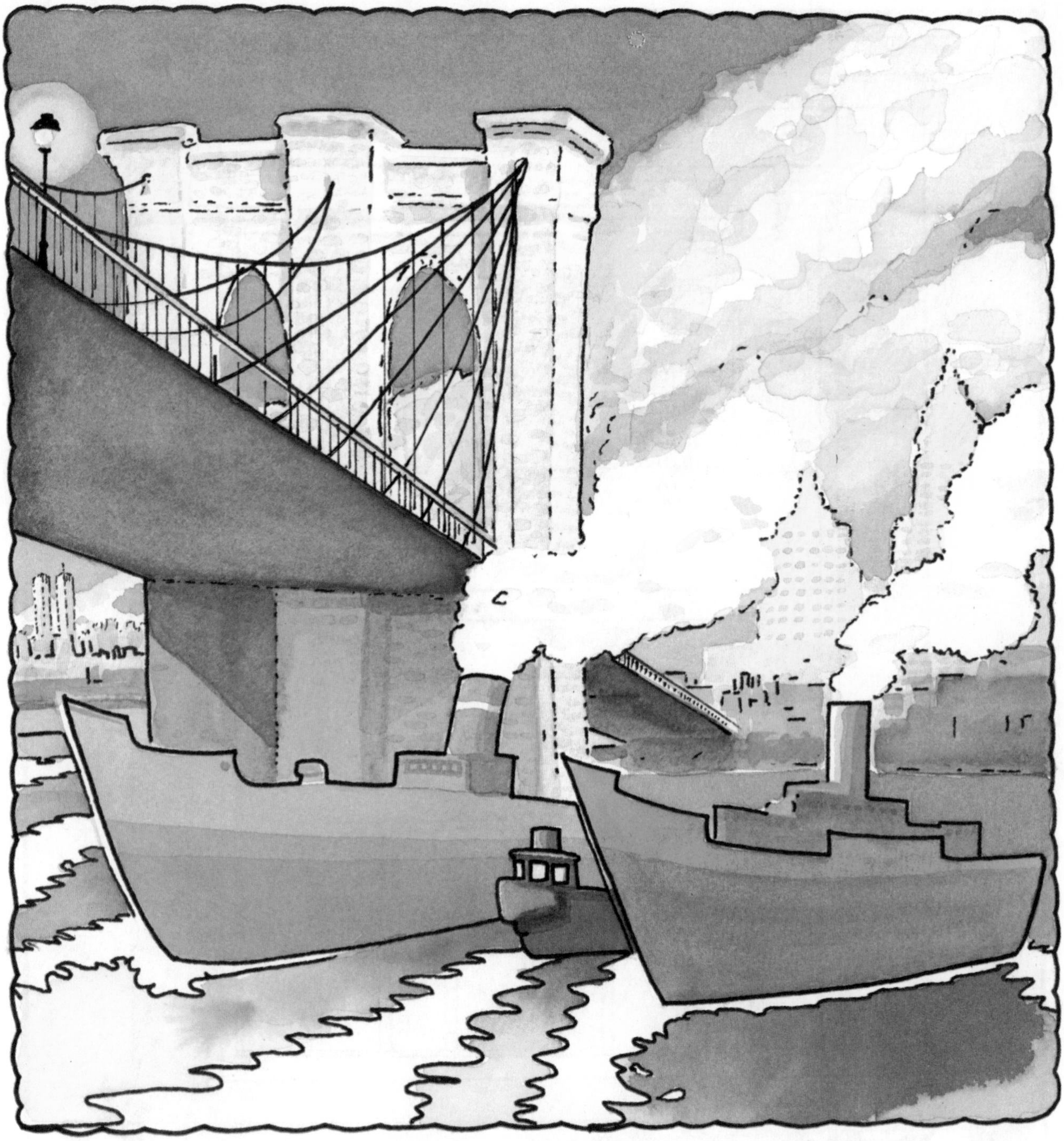

There are many beautiful views in Brooklyn.

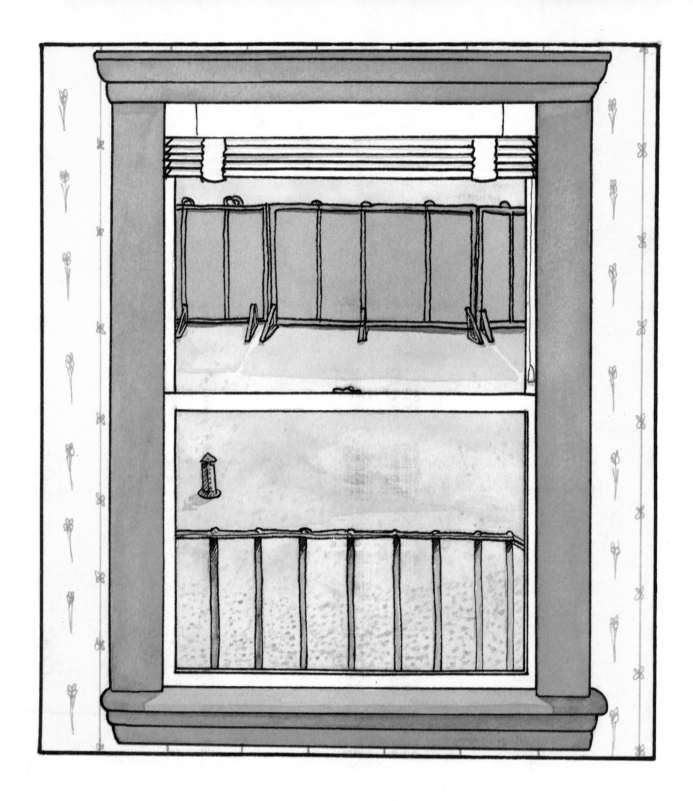

The view from Mrs. Fitz's apartment window isn't one of them. Outside her kitchen window are a fire escape, a sagging tar-paper roof, and the back sides of some billboards.

One day at a gate sale on Pineapple Street, Mrs. Fitz bought two pink flamingos for three dollars.

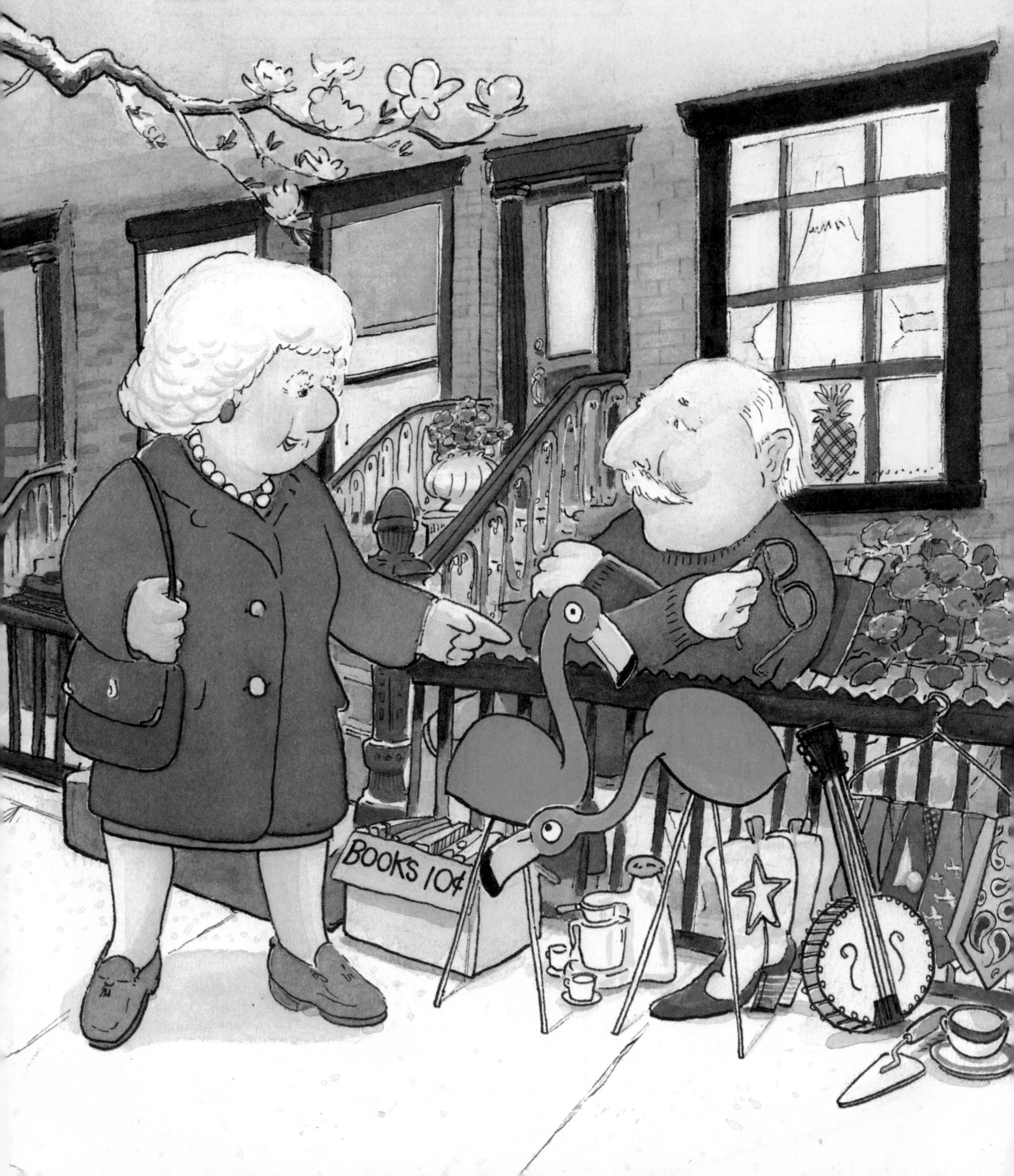
BOOKS 10¢

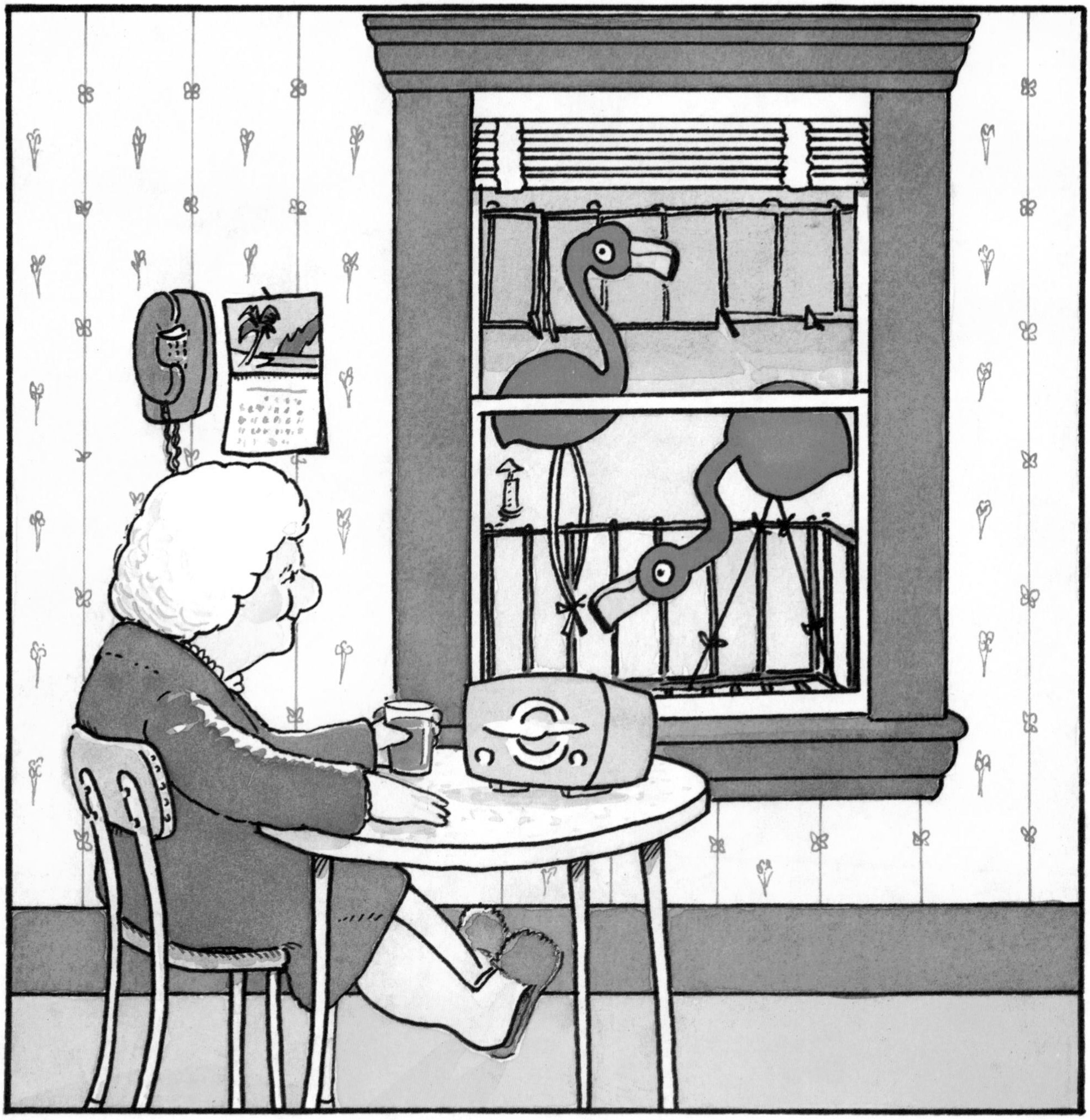

At home she tied them to the railing of her fire escape.

The next morning Mrs. Fitz squeezed fresh orange juice. She found some lovely big-band music on the radio and sat looking at the pink flamingos for a long time. It was a most pleasant morning.

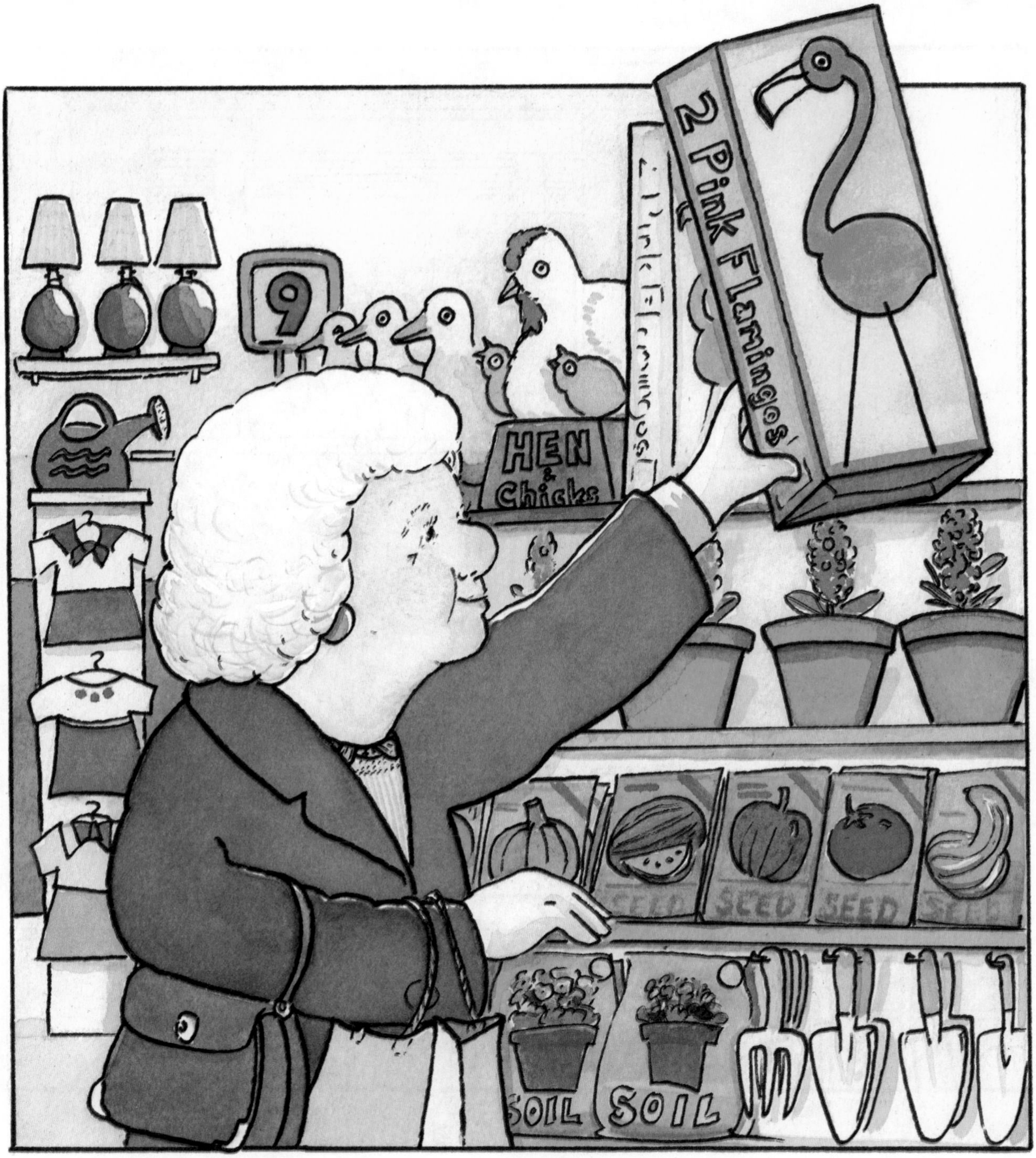
2 Pink Flamingos
9
HEN & Chicks
SEED
SEED
SEED
SOIL
SOIL

That Thursday when she got paid, she stopped at the five-and-ten and bought two more flamingos to put on her fire escape beside the first two.

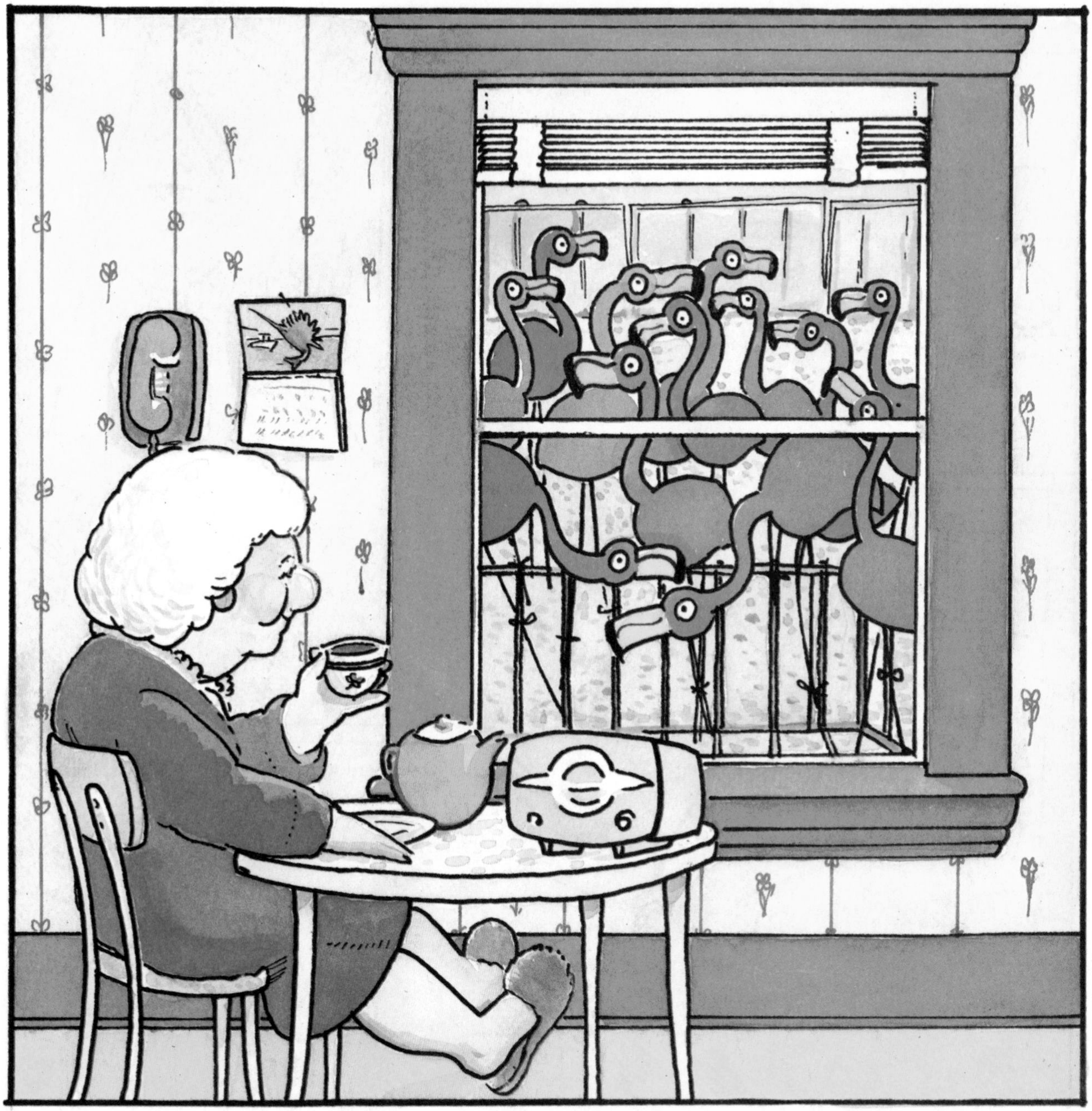

Mrs. Fitz was very pleased with her improved view. She enjoyed it in the morning when she drank her orange juice, and in the evening when she drank a cup of tea.

Every Thursday she bought another pair of flamingos, until she had twelve.

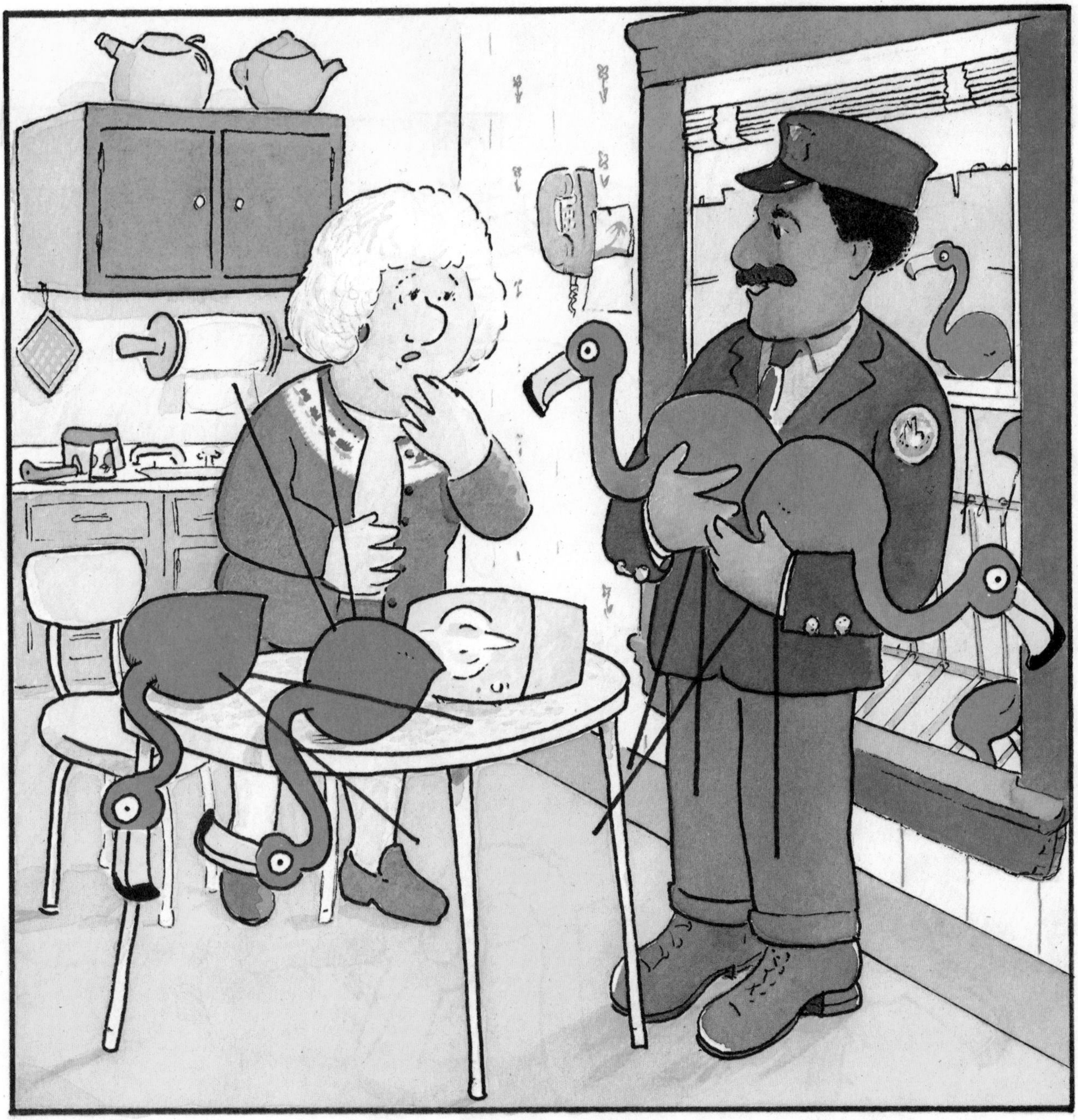

A nice young fireman named Mr. Moore was making safety inspections in the neighborhood one day. He told Mrs. Fitz that it was illegal to attach anything to a fire escape. He helped her bring the flamingos inside.

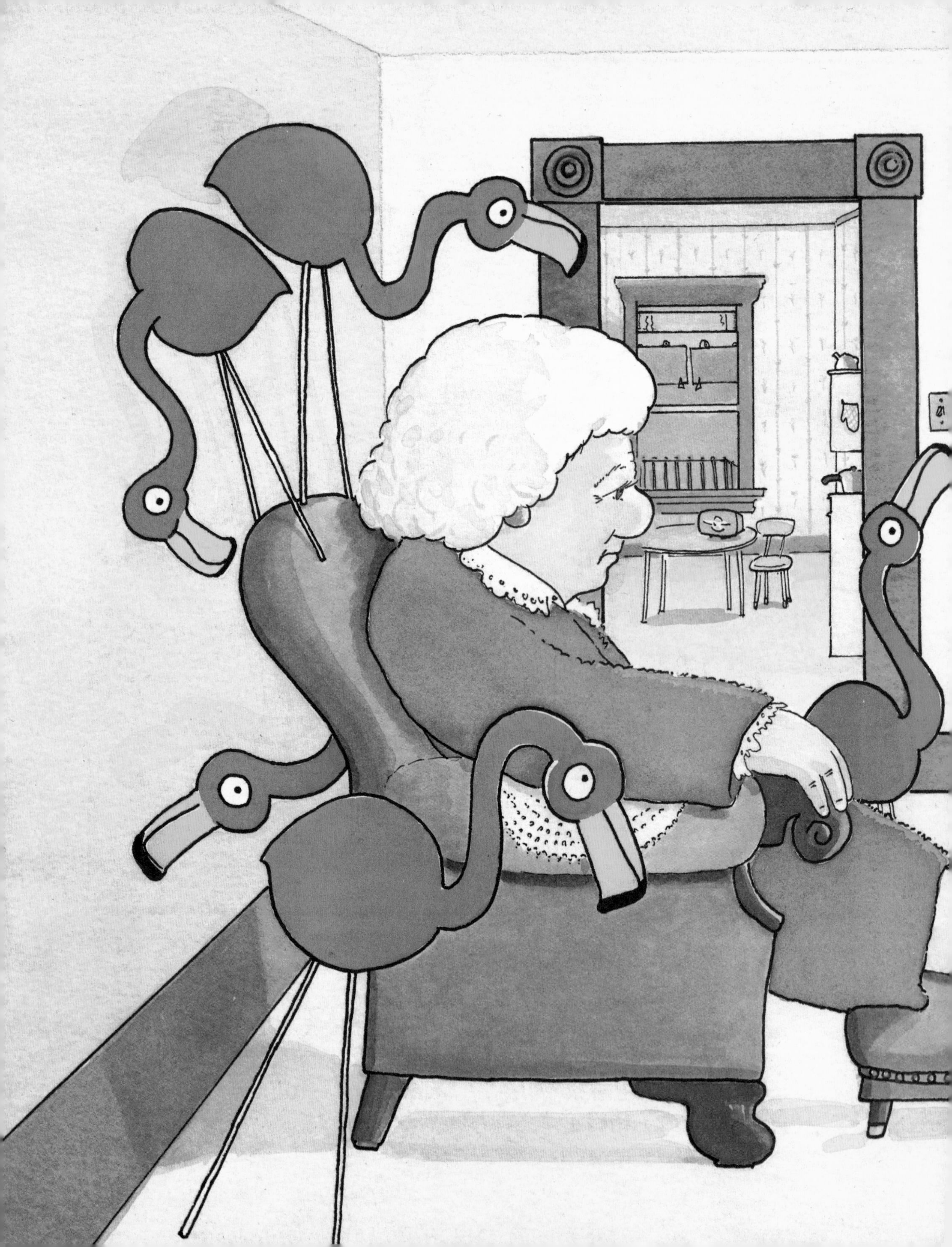

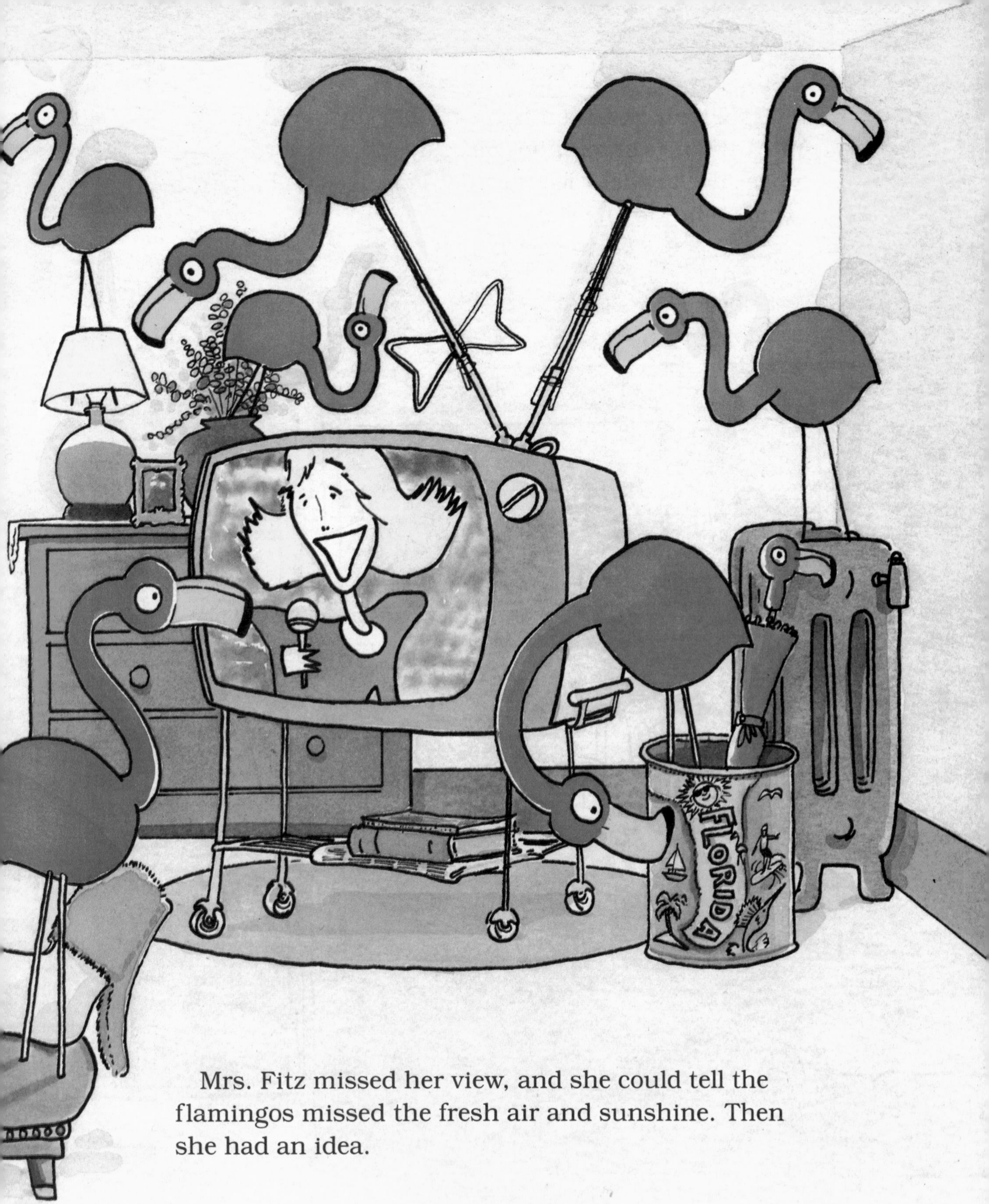
FLORIDA

Mrs. Fitz missed her view, and she could tell the flamingos missed the fresh air and sunshine. Then she had an idea.

Mrs. Fitz took a flamingo with her and went to Mr. Anthony's shoe shop. She had Mr. Anthony make special sticky feet for the flamingos so they could stand up anywhere.

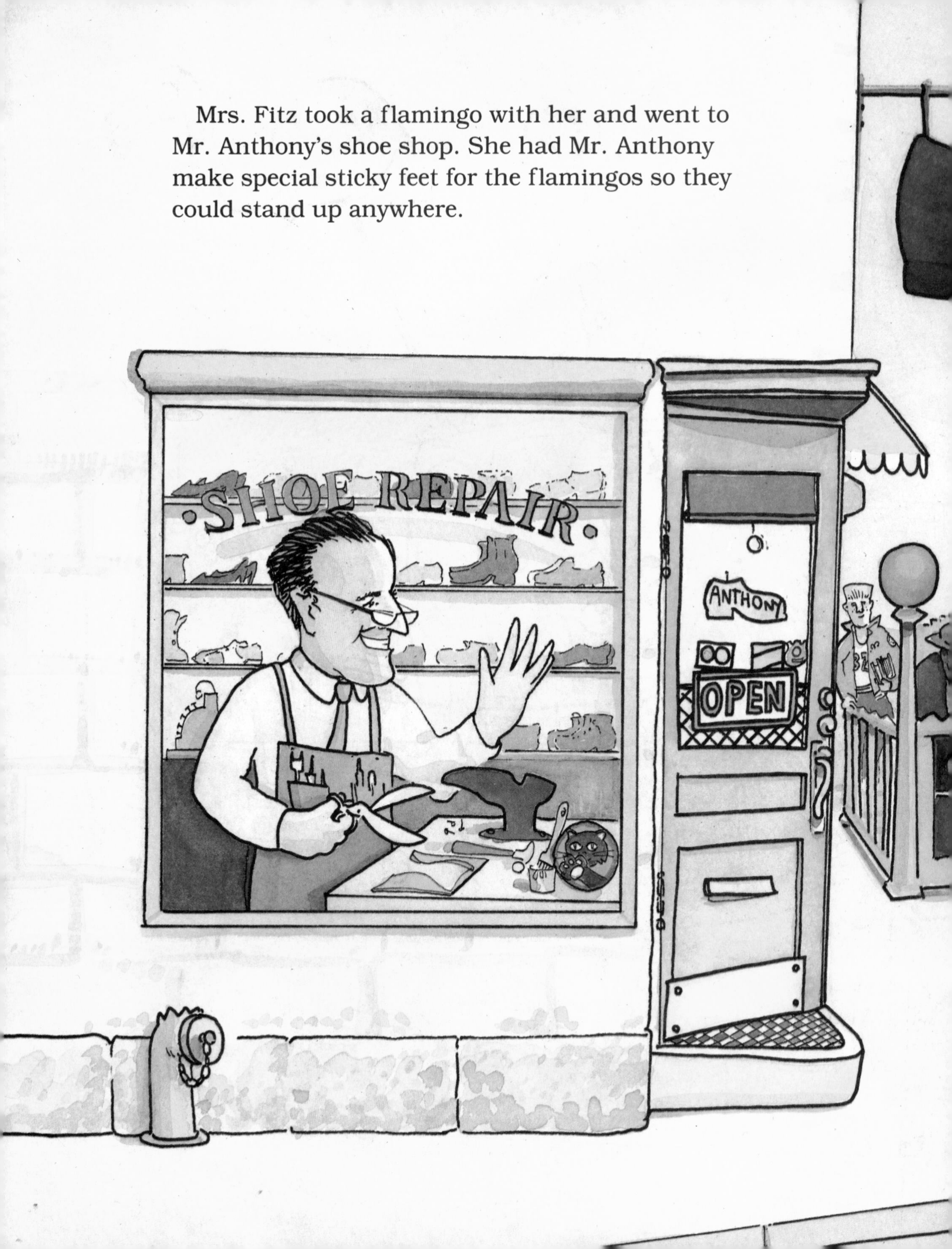
SHOE REPAIR
ANTHONY
OPEN

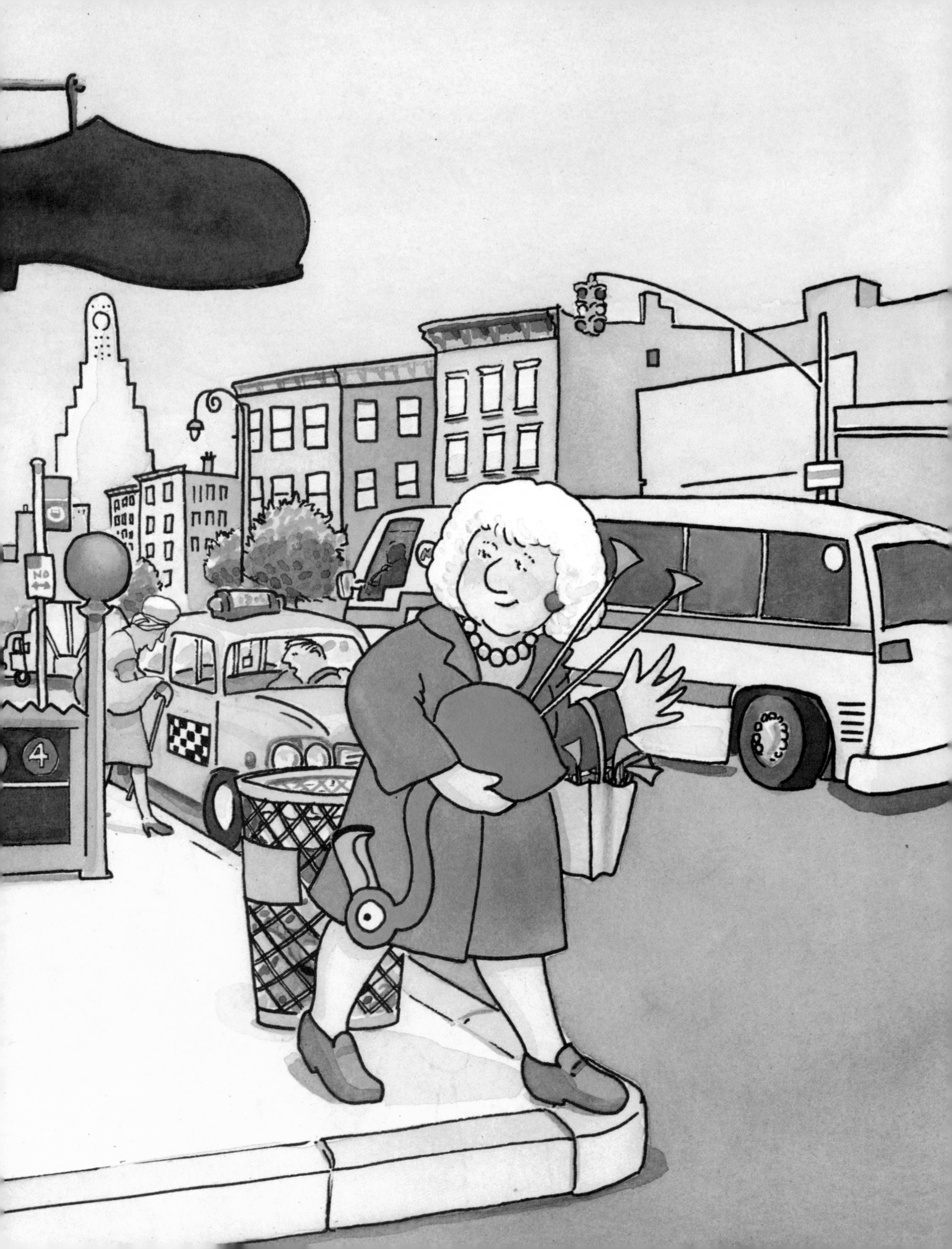
NO
4

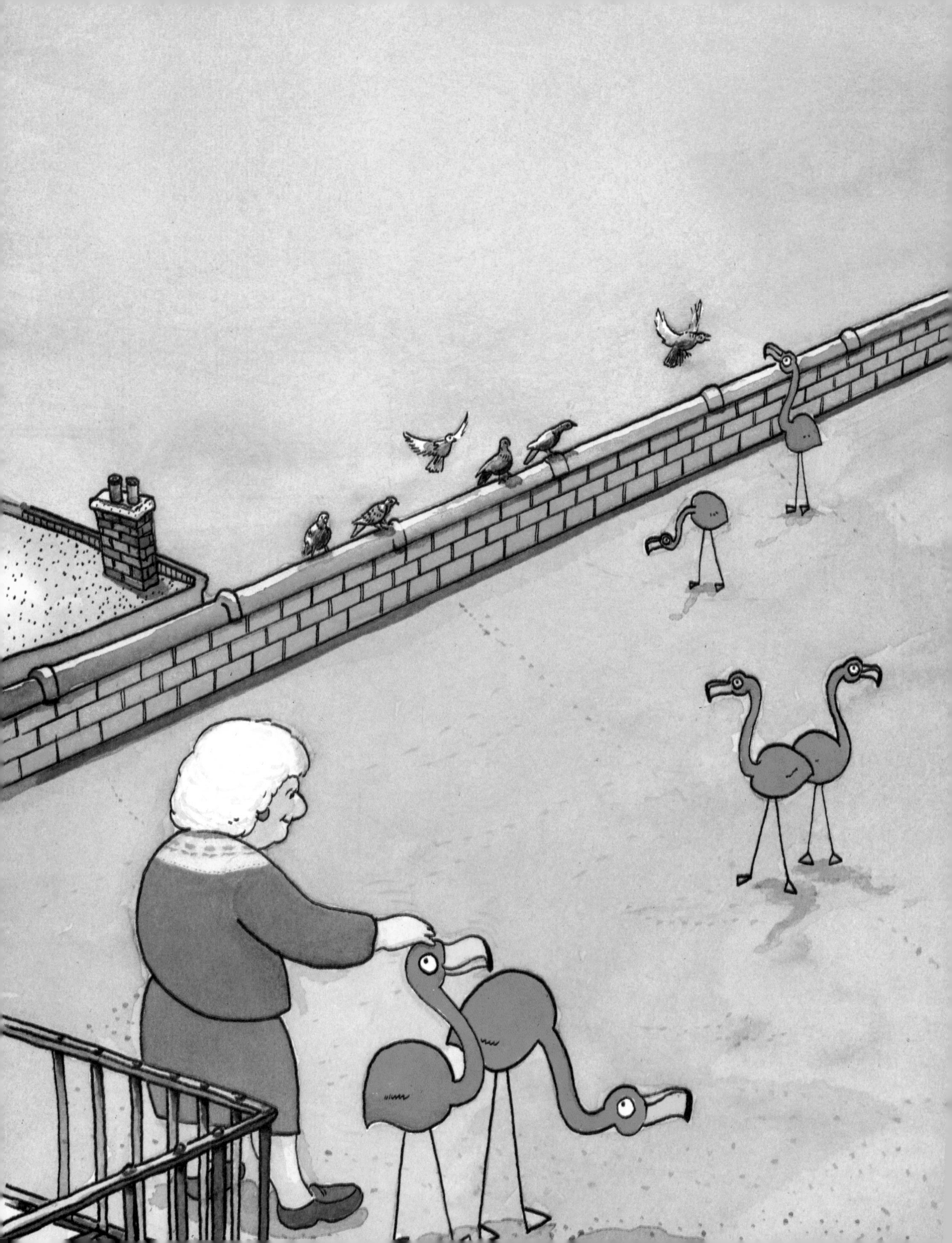

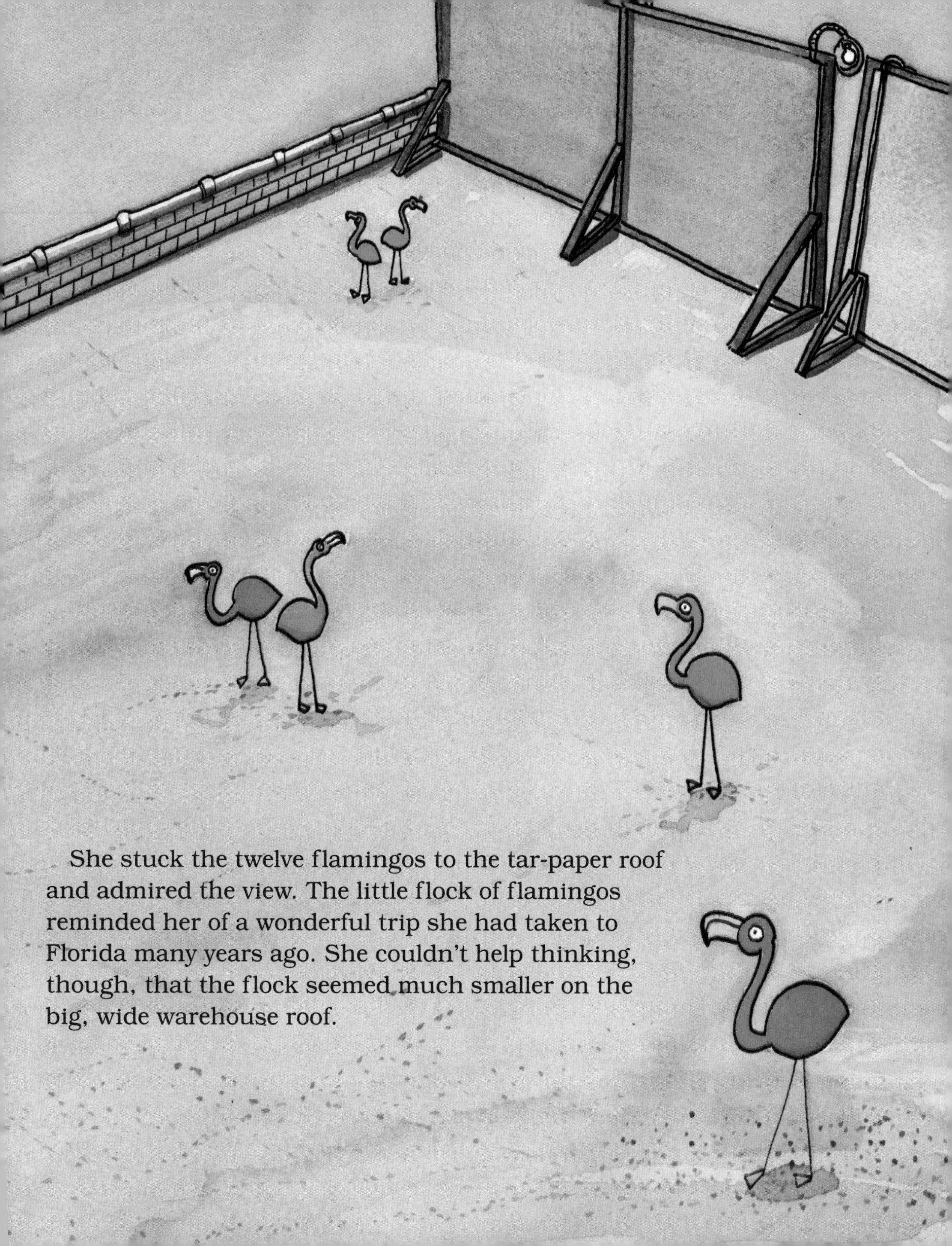

She stuck the twelve flamingos to the tar-paper roof and admired the view. The little flock of flamingos reminded her of a wonderful trip she had taken to Florida many years ago. She couldn't help thinking, though, that the flock seemed much smaller on the big, wide warehouse roof.

Every Thursday Mrs. Fitz got two more flamingos. Soon she had a really big flock on the roof.

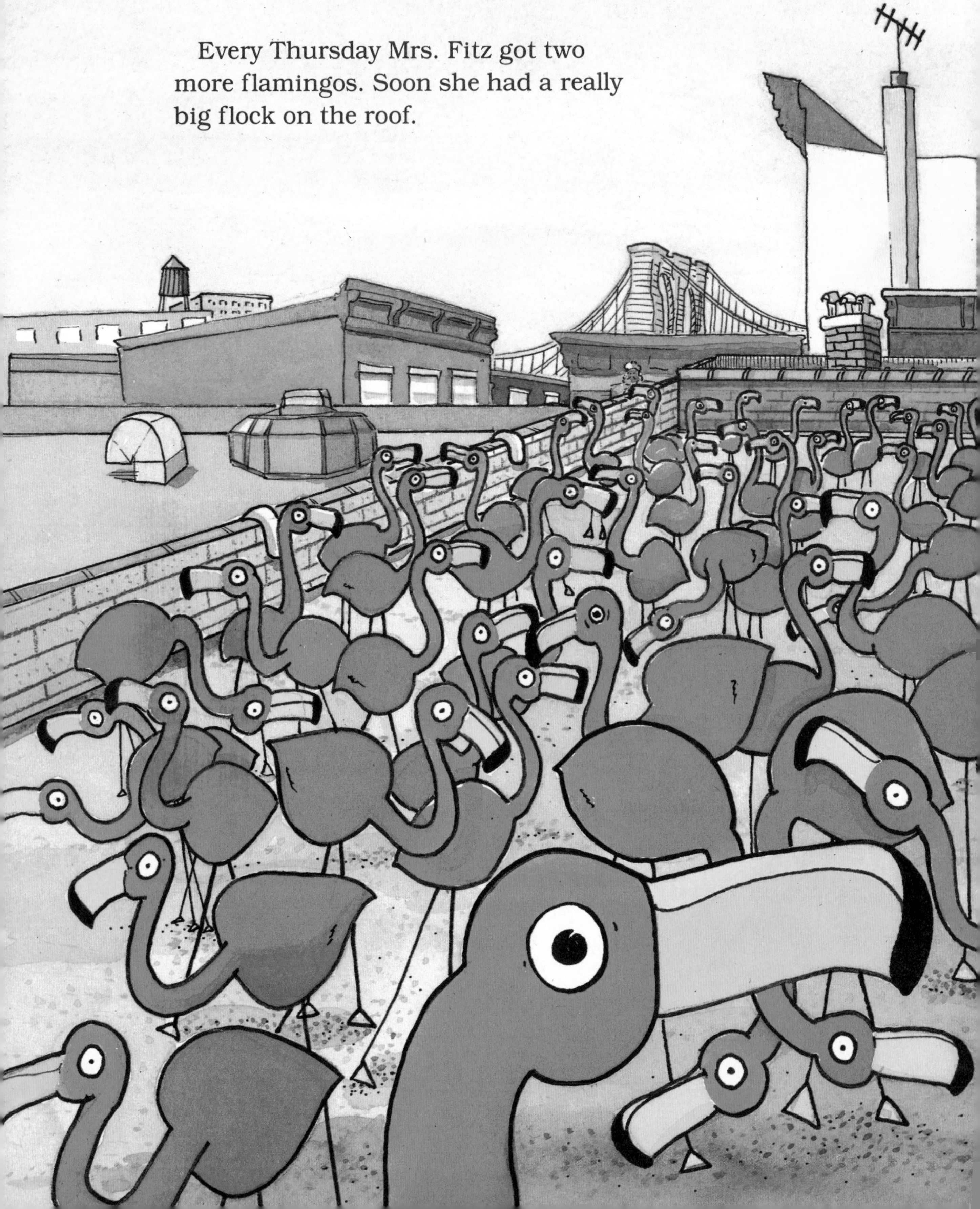

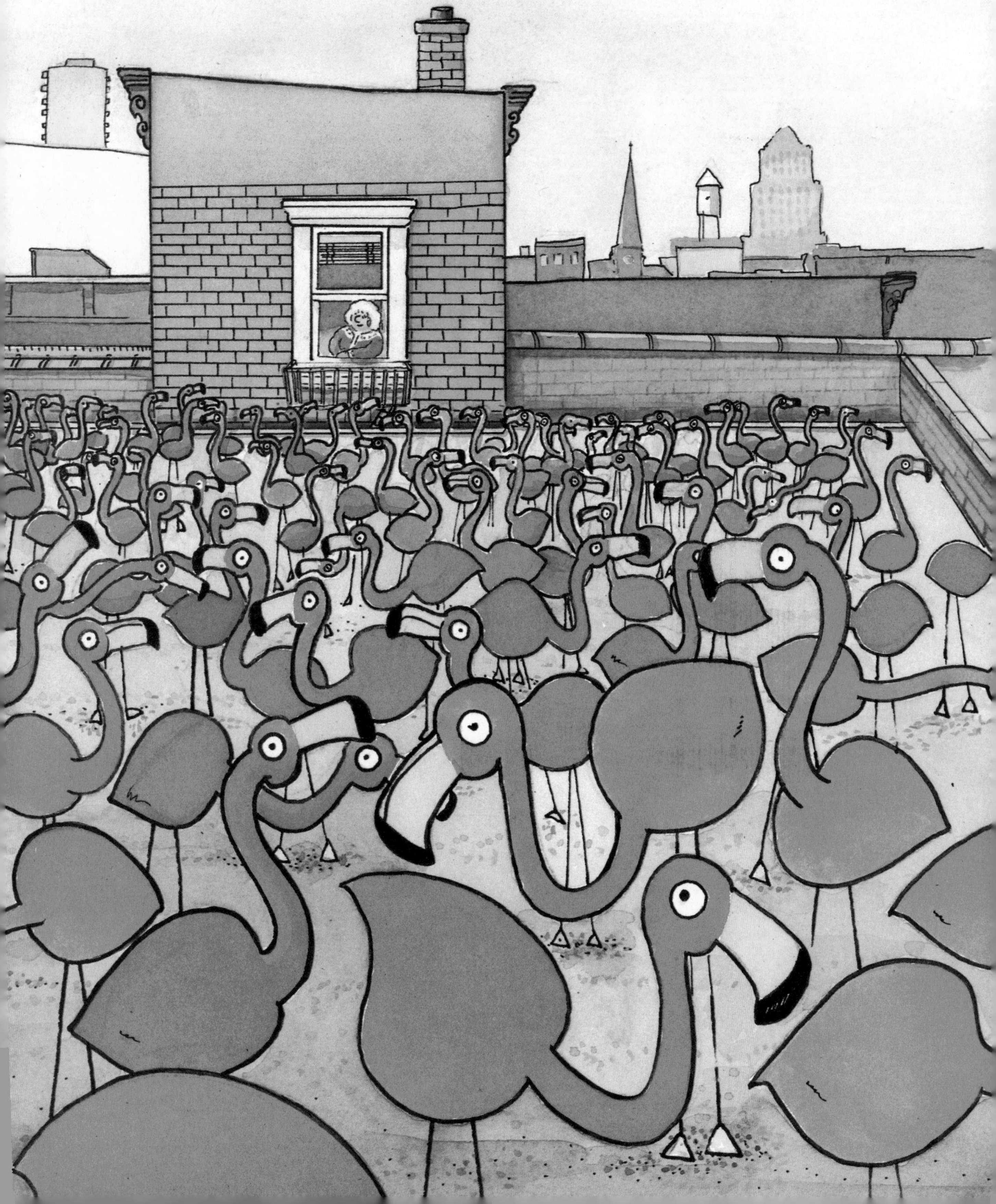

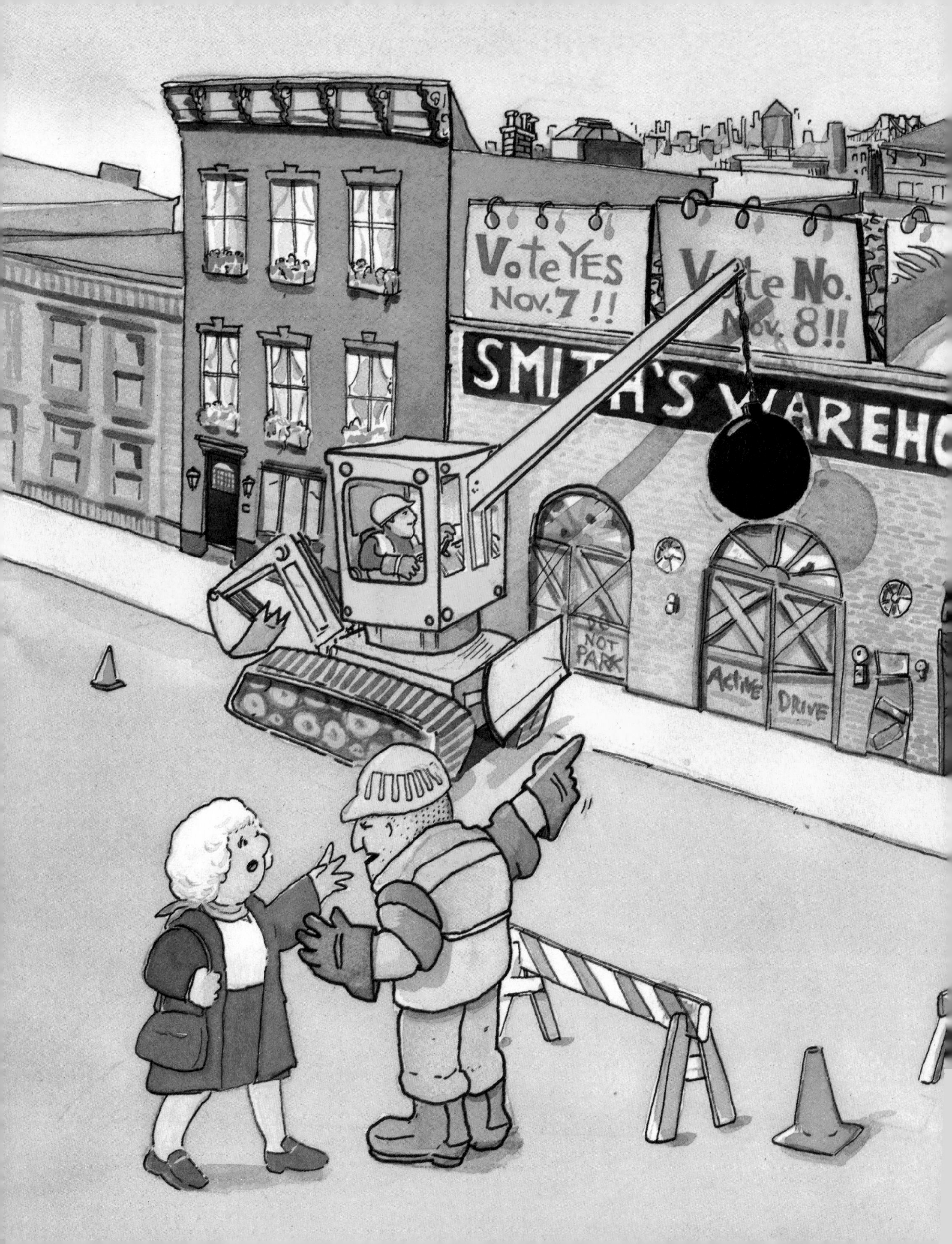
Vote YES Nov. 7 !!
Vote No. Nov. 8!!
SMITH'S WAREHO
DO NOT PARK
Active DRIVE

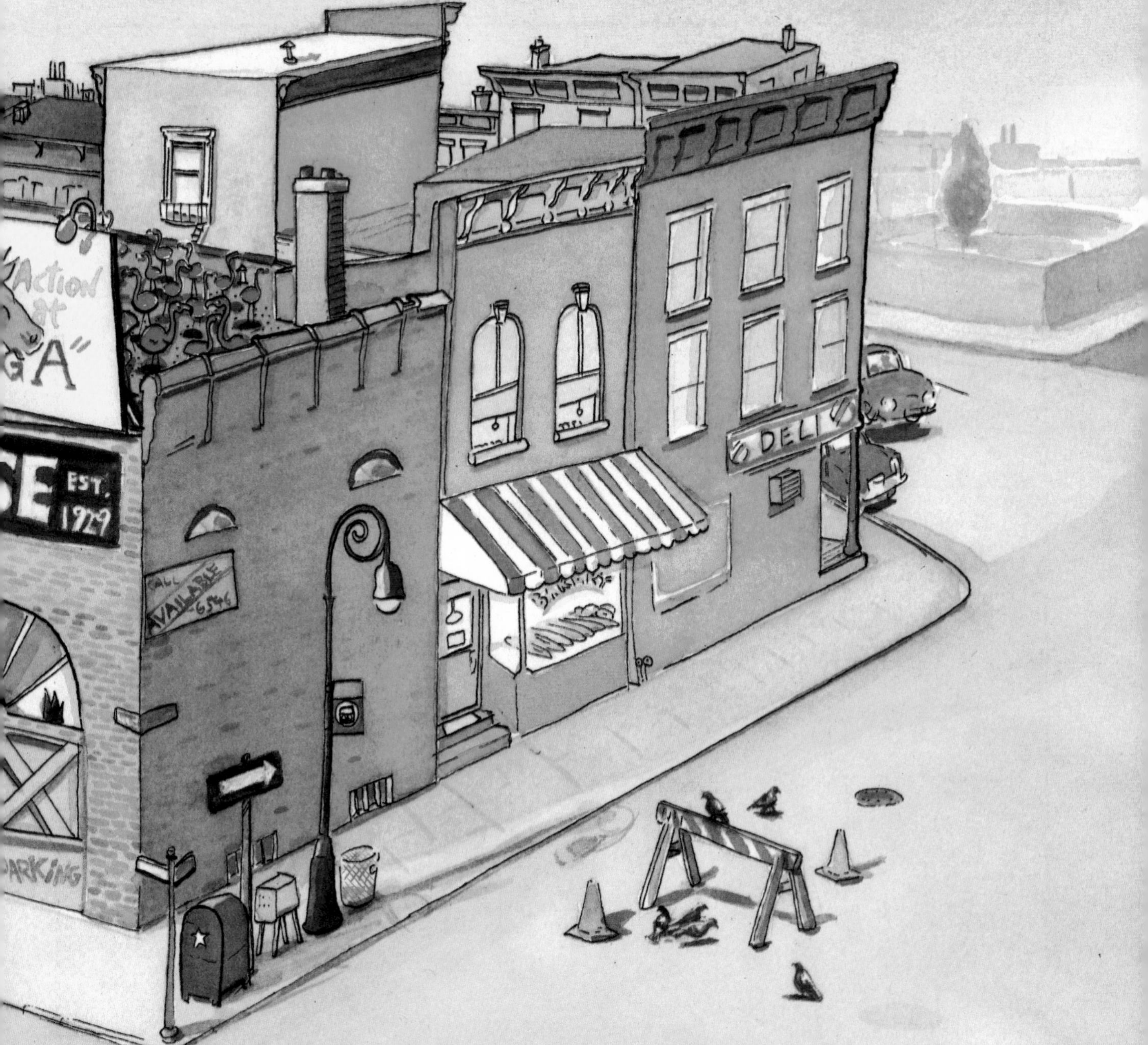
Action at
EST. 1929
CALL
AVAILABLE
DELI

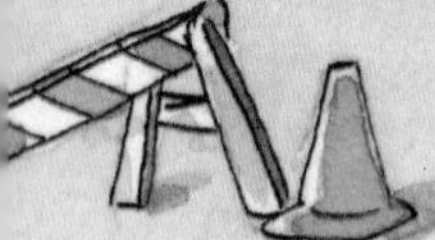

One evening on her way home, Mrs. Fitz saw a wrecking crew preparing to knock down a building around the corner from her apartment. It was the warehouse with her flamingos on its roof!

"Stop!" she screamed. "You can't tear down that building. Oh, my flamingos!"

"Stand back, lady," said the foreman. "This building is unsafe. We're knocking it down right now!"

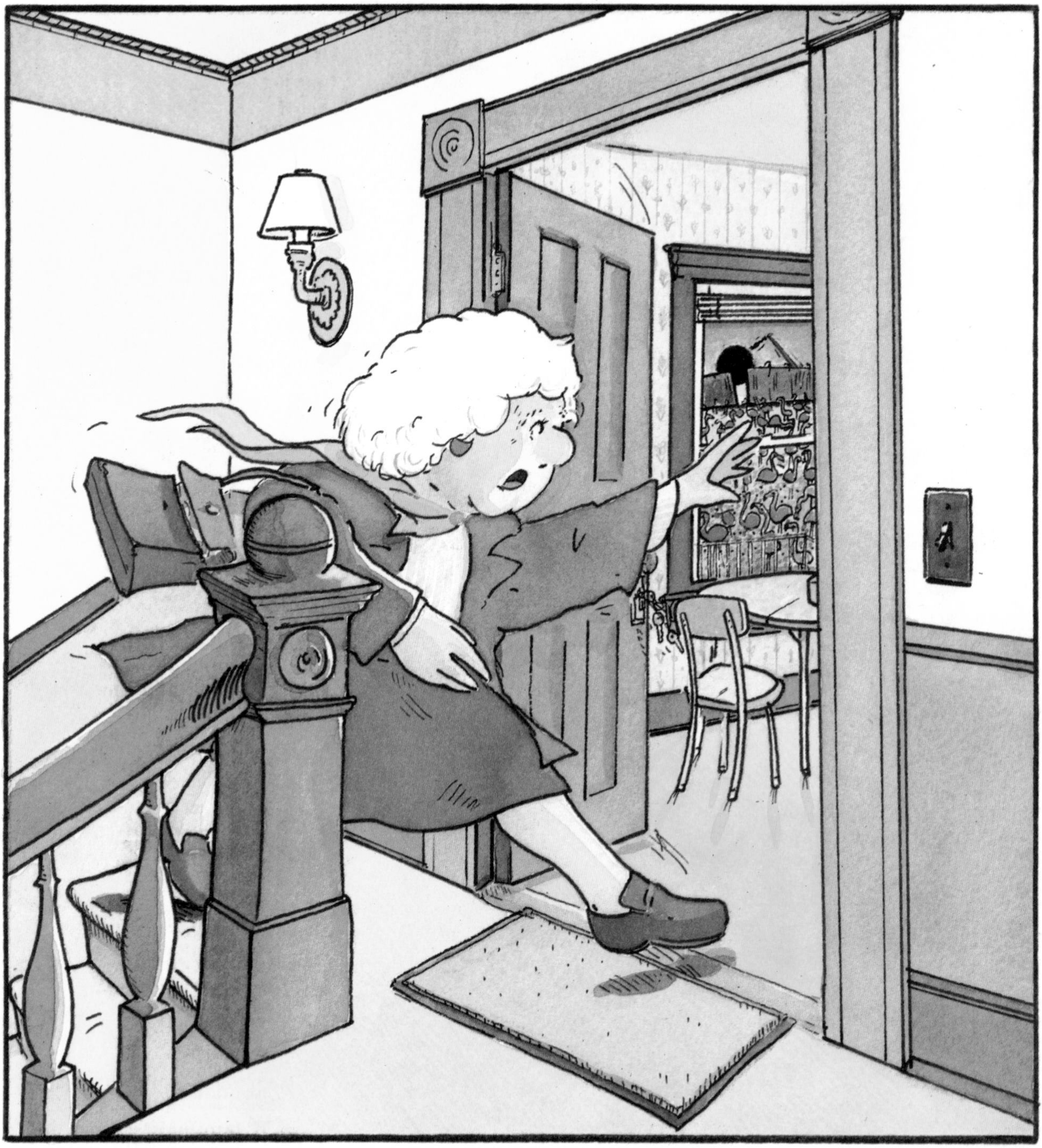

Mrs. Fitz raced around the corner and up the stairs into her apartment. She threw open the kitchen window and started to climb out, but—

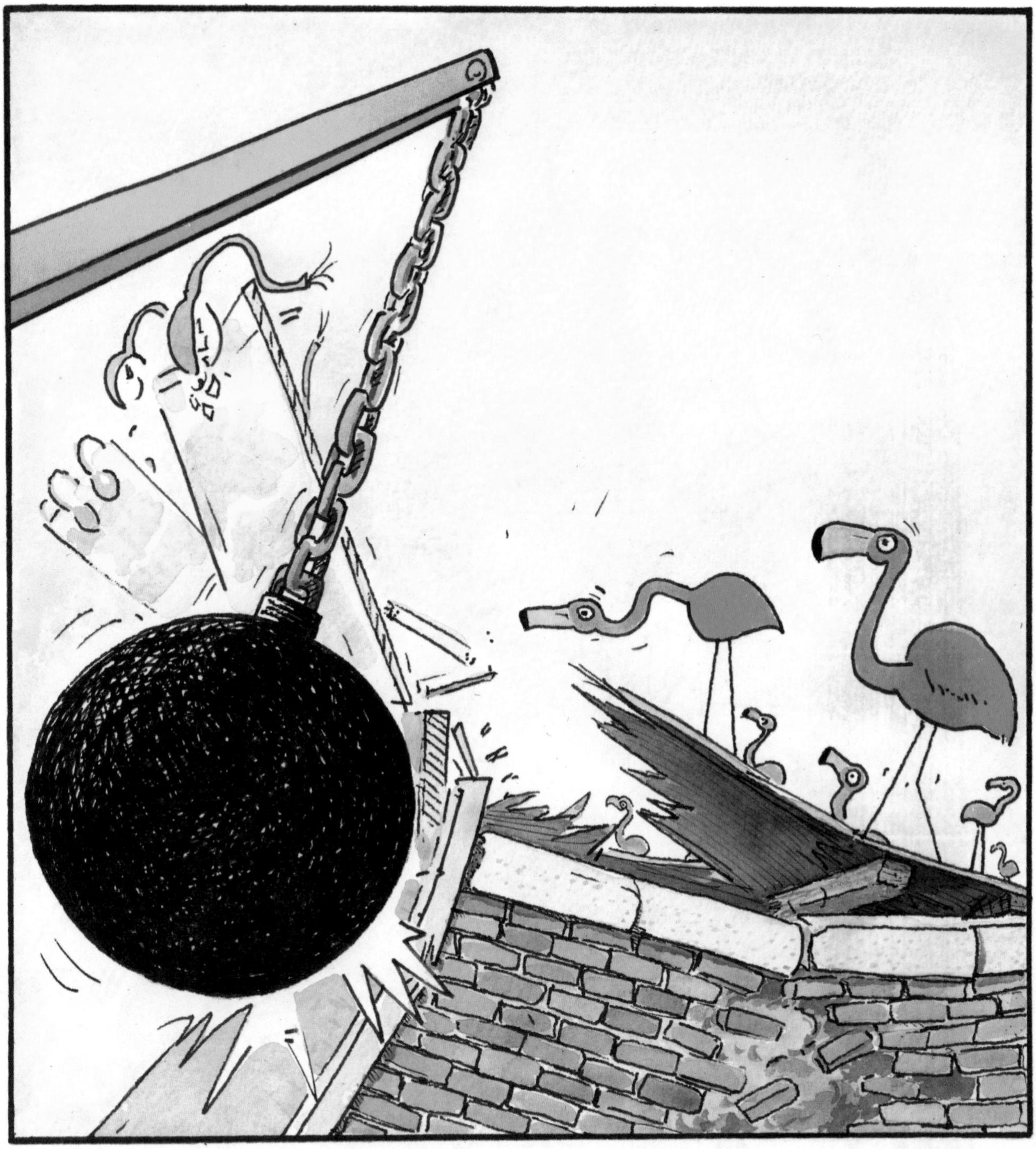

BOOOOM! It was too late. The wrecking ball hit the building.

BOOOOM! The roof began to shake.

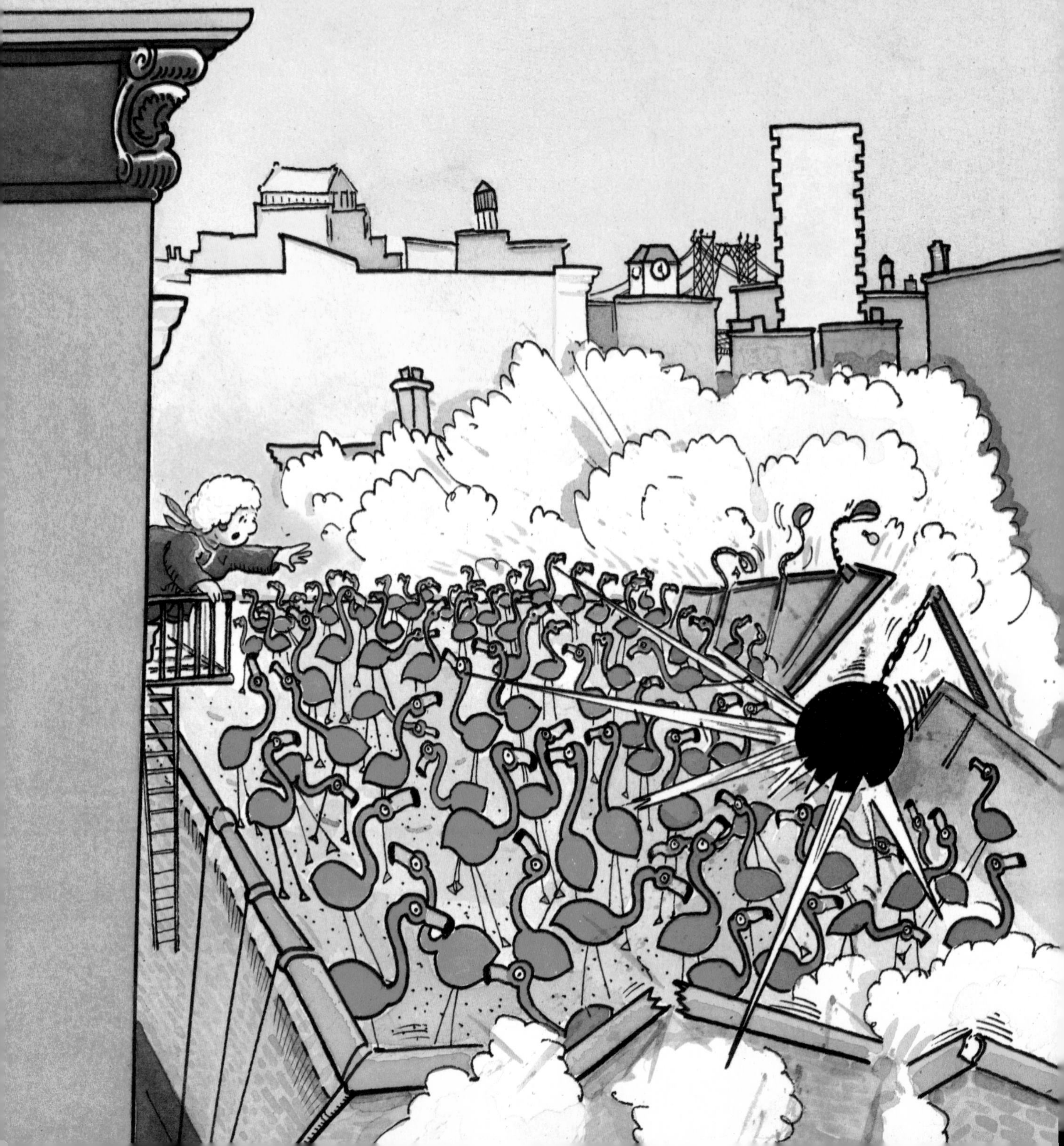

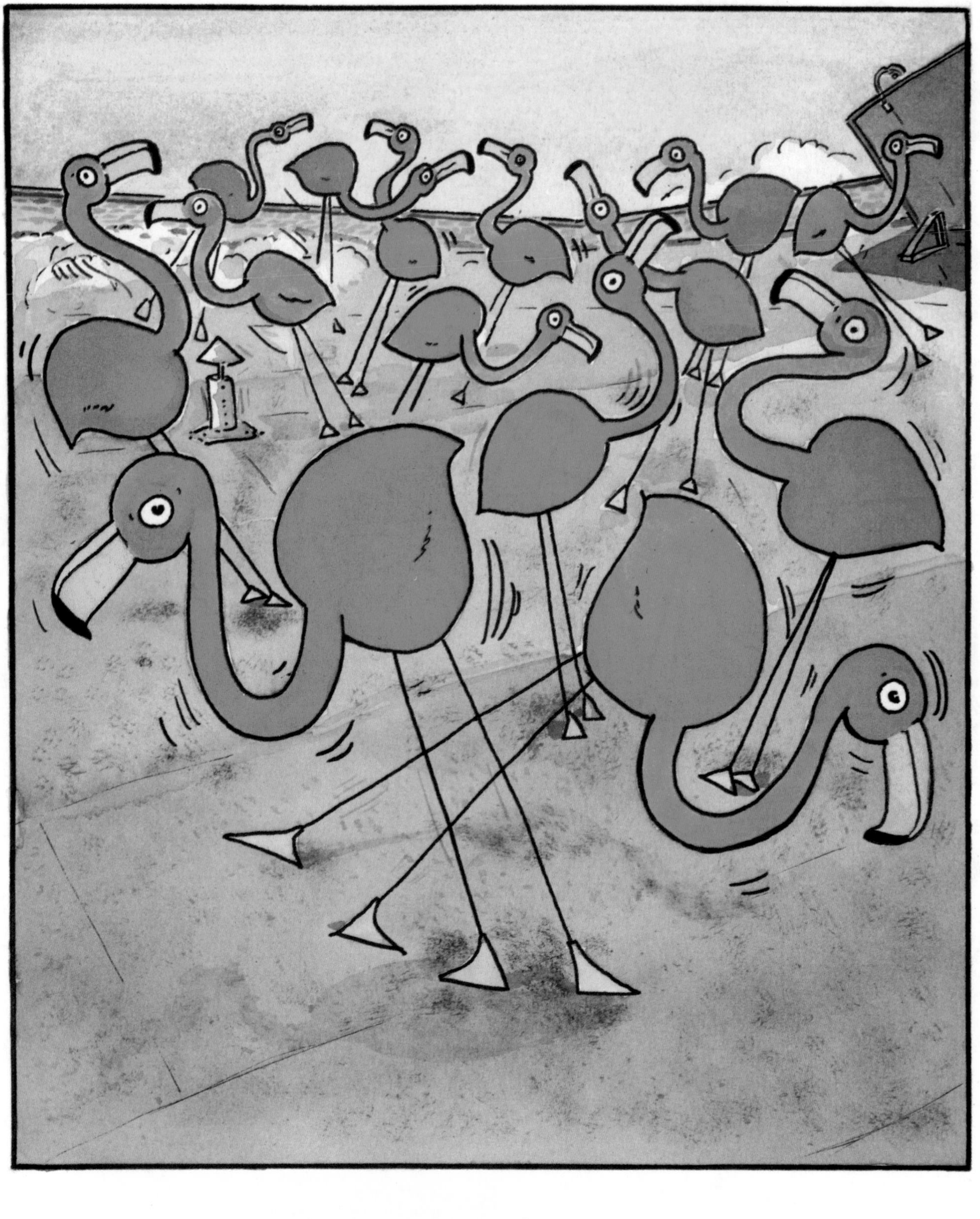

BOOOOM! The flamingos began to shake.

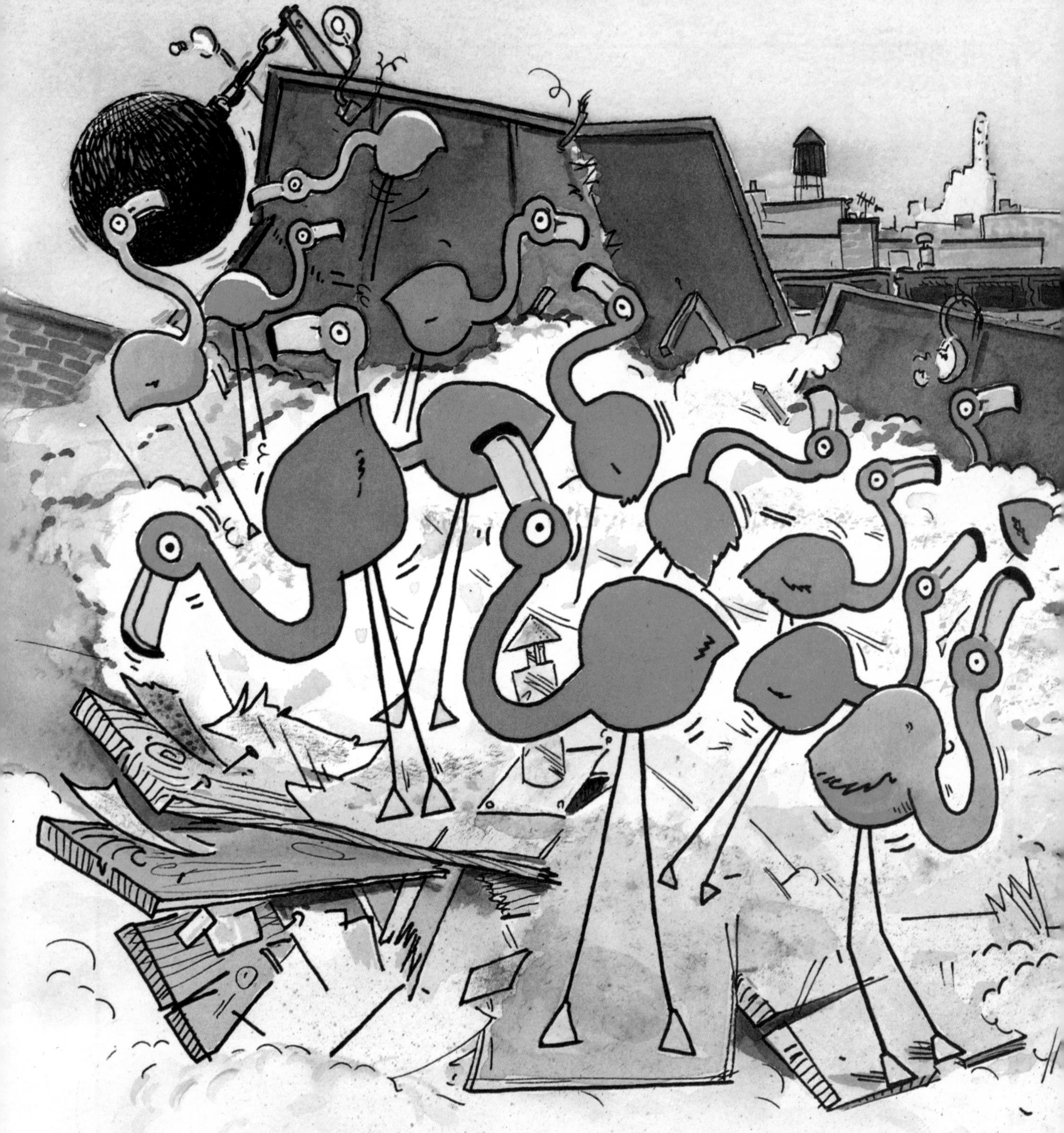

BOOOOM! The roof began to fall.

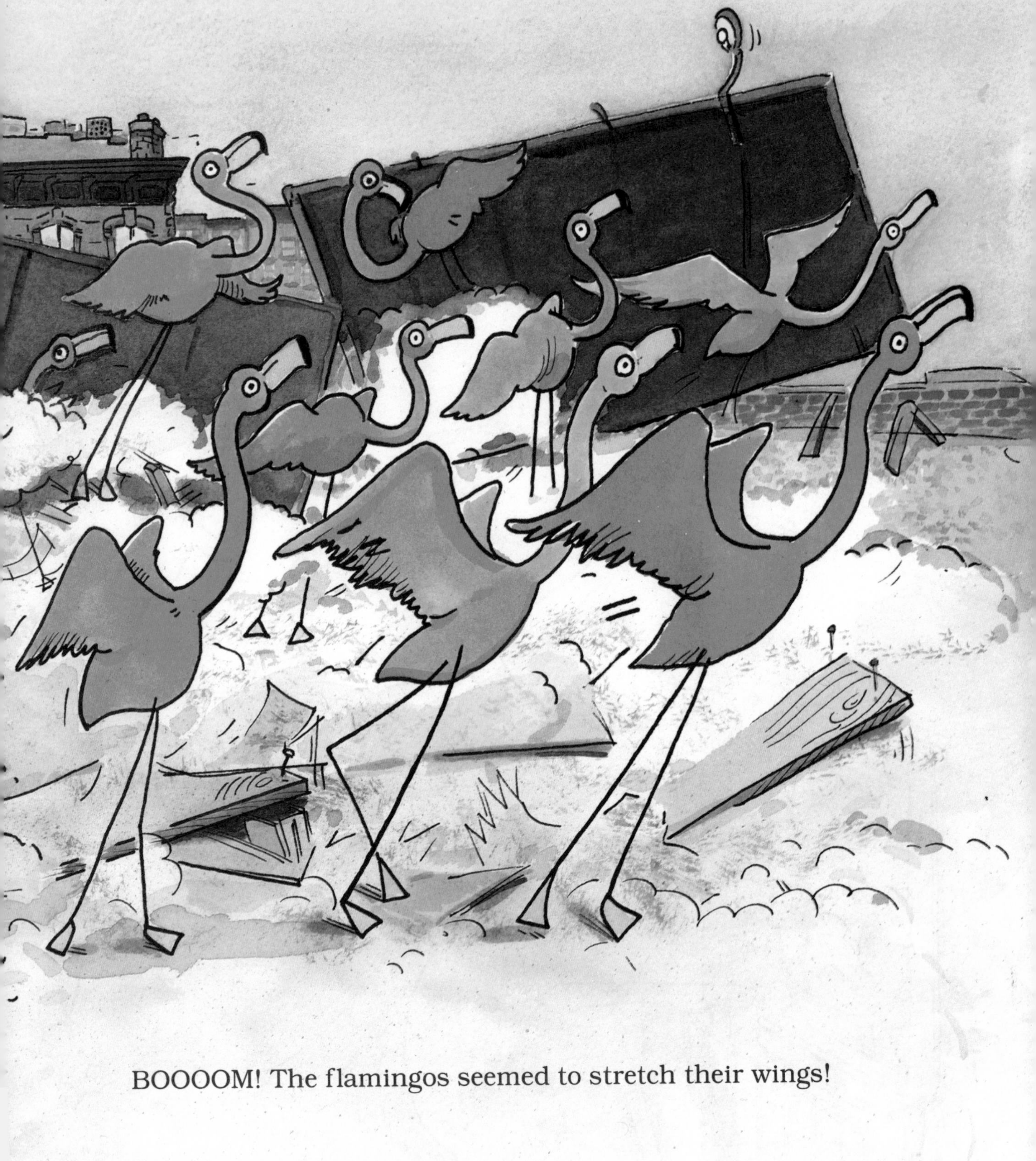

BOOOOM! The flamingos seemed to stretch their wings!

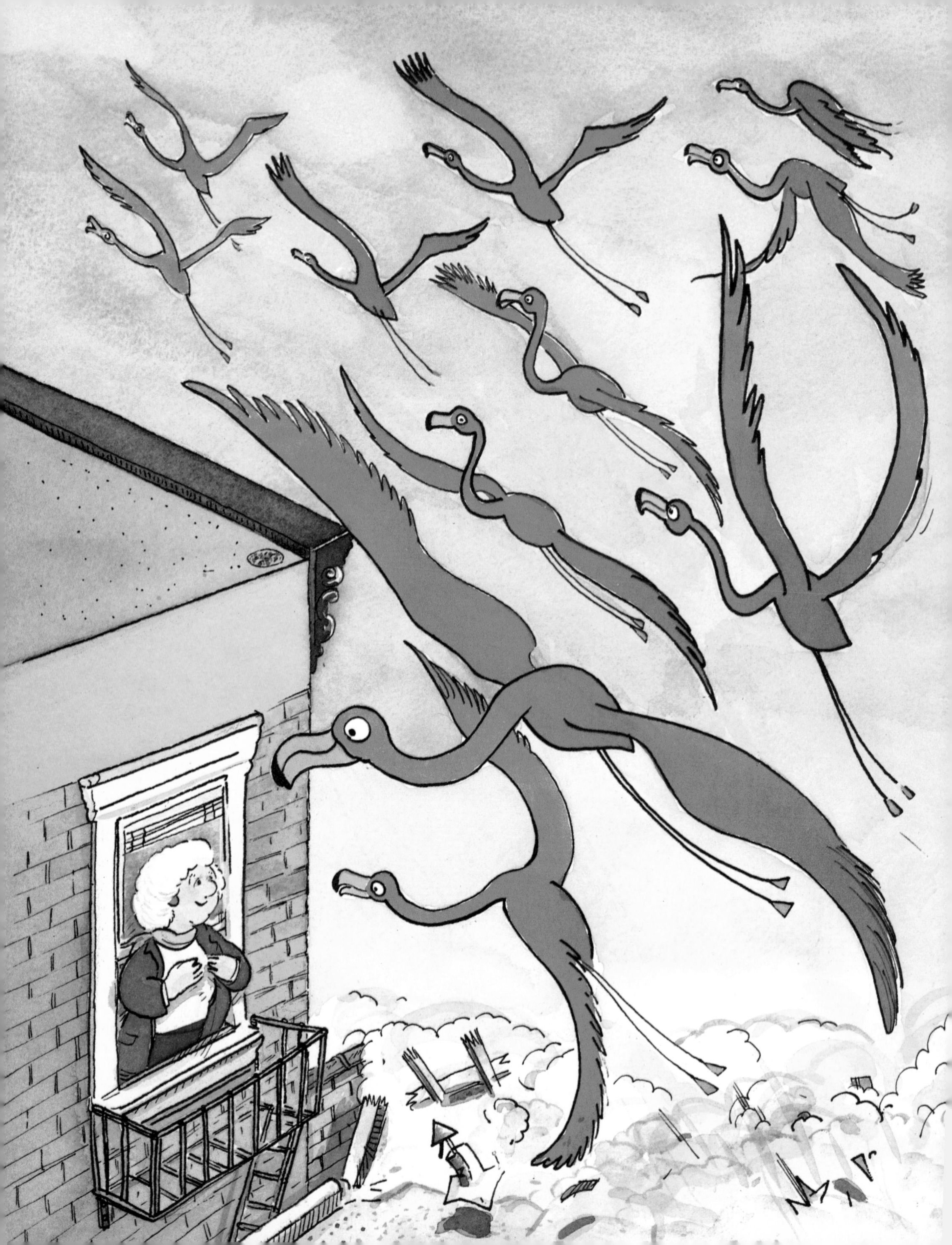

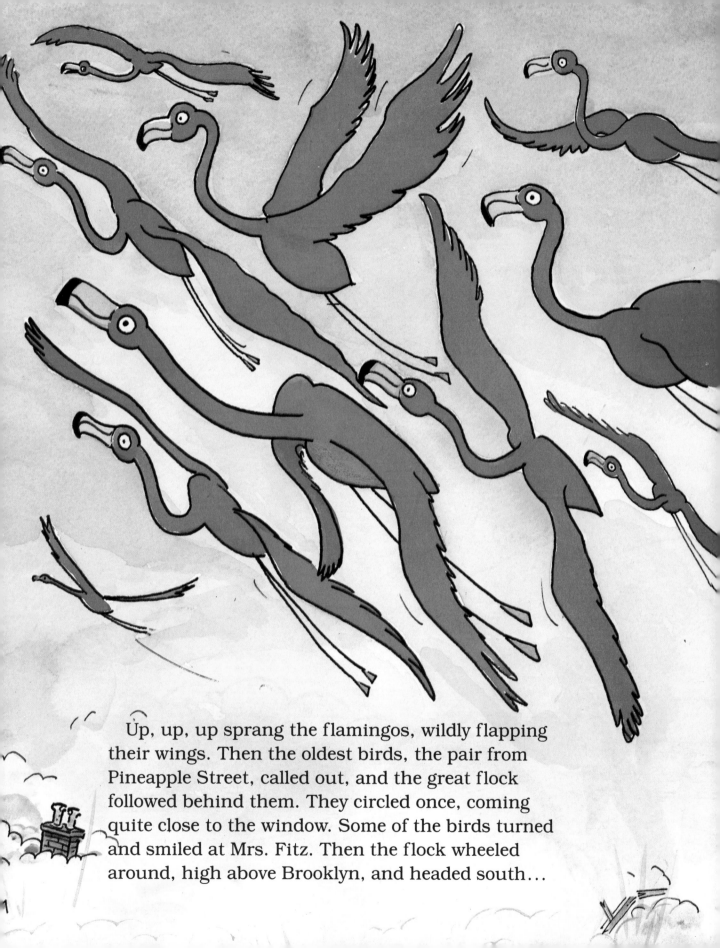

Up, up, up sprang the flamingos, wildly flapping
their wings. Then the oldest birds, the pair from
Pineapple Street, called out, and the great flock
followed behind them. They circled once, coming
quite close to the window. Some of the birds turned
and smiled at Mrs. Fitz. Then the flock wheeled
around, high above Brooklyn, and headed south…

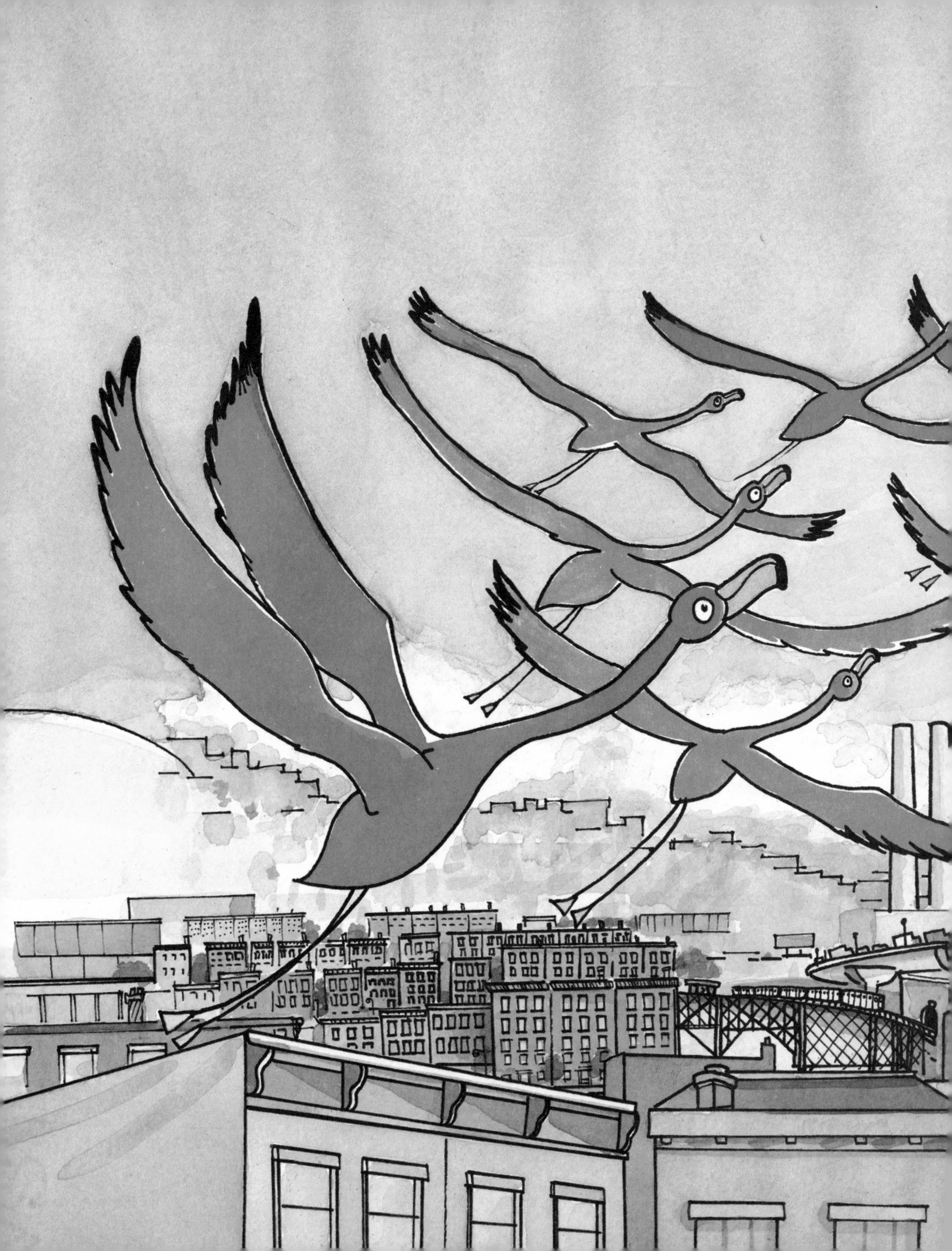